SCOOBY-DOO!

FRANKEN CREEPY

adapted by Kate Howard
from the script by Jim Krieg

SCHOLASTIC INC.

ISBN 978-0-545-67528-4

10 9 8 7 6 5 4 3 2 1

14 15 16 17 18 19/0

Printed in the U.S.A.   40
First printing, August 2014

"*Hola*, Daphne fans!" Daphne Blake said into her webcam. "It's time for *Jeepers! It's Daphne!* Fred, Velma, Shaggy, Scooby, and I have solved tons of mysteries. Check out our greatest hits!"

WATCH NOW!!!

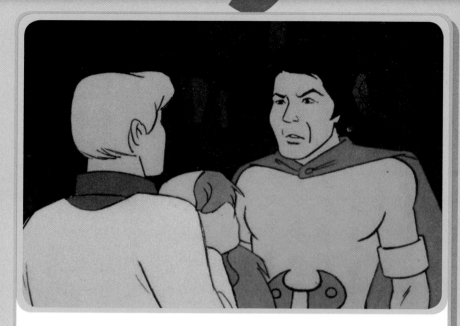

"We unmasked Mamba Wamba, a music producer pretending to be a creepy witch doctor.

"Velma solved the case of Creeps and Crawls, a pair of lawyers dressed up as phantoms!

"Mama Mione stirred up all kinds of trouble when she pretended to be Old Ironface.

"And who could ever forget the time C. L. Magnus dressed up as Redbeard's ghost?"

When the webcast ended, the kids headed to Velma's great-uncle Baron Basil's castle in Transylvania. The baron had left her the castle in his will.

"Anyone who gets close to the castle will lose what they love most," said Cuthbert Crawley, Velma's family lawyer. "It's cursed!"

"I don't believe in curses," Velma said.

The gang got another warning — from the baron's ghost! He blew the Mystery Machine into pieces.

Shaggy and Scooby were scared. They didn't want to go to the castle.

"We have to go. He killed my van!" Fred sobbed. "This time, it's personal."

The gang hopped aboard the creepy
Transylvanian Express.

"Ri rove ris train!" Scooby barked. "Two
words: rack bar!"

But the food was just as creepy as the train.
"Blood pudding, goat's-head pie, wolf-paw tart?"
Scooby stuck out his tongue. "Ruck!"

8

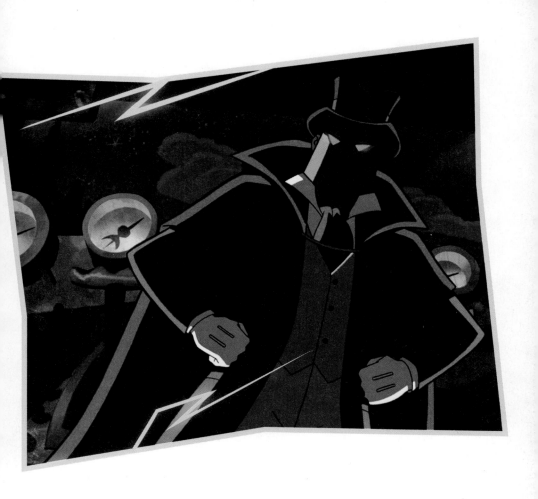

Velma told the gang her secret. Her family's name wasn't always Dinkley. It used to be —

"Von Dinkenstein?" the others gasped.

"Yes." Velma sighed. "Von Dinkenstein: the man who created a monster. His story inspired the book *Frankenstein*!"

Suddenly, the train sped out of control. The ghost of the baron had taken over!

"You didn't listen to my warning! Beware the Von Dinkenstein curse!" the ghost cackled.

The train crashed into the station in Transylvania. No one was hurt, but everyone was scared — especially when an angry mob surrounded the gang.

"You!" they yelled, pointing at Velma. "You're not welcome in this town!"

"Come with me," a tiny, hunched man said. "All of you. Me Iago."

While Iago drove the gang to the castle, he told them about the Von Dinkenstein monster. The people had feared the monster, so they destroyed it.

"My master vowed revenge," Iago said. "He cursed town for all eternity."

Shaggy gulped. "Like, that's a long time!"

At the castle, the gang got a tour from the housekeeper, Mrs. Vanders. "Let me show you the laboratory!" she said.

"Scooby and I will take a closer look inside that freezer for snacks," Shaggy said.

"I must inform you of two facts. One, that is not food," Mrs. Vanders said. "Those are parts the baron rejected for his creature."

"Zoinks!" Shaggy yelped. "Like, what's the other fact?"

Mrs. Vanders pulled the tablecloth away. The table was actually a giant block of ice...with a monster frozen inside!

"I'll prove this monster is a fake!" Velma screamed. "I'll try to recreate my uncle's monster. I'll prove monsters don't exist!"

Fred, Daphne, Shaggy, and Scooby headed into town. Shaggy saw a sign that made his mouth water. "Eating contest? Like, count us in!"

Shaggy and Scooby-Doo won the contest. "To reward you, here are two sets of lederhosen," said Mayor Burgermeister.

Shaggy and Scooby put on their new outfits. For the first time in their lives, they felt full!

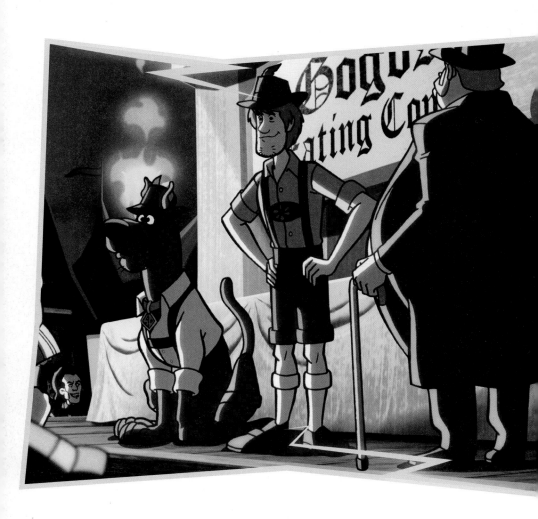

Meanwhile, Daphne was doing a little shopping.

"This is adorable!" she said, squeezing into a dress. Daphne suddenly looked huge and swollen. "Jeepers! What's up with my hair?"

Shaggy and Scooby were full. Daphne didn't feel beautiful. Fred was still crying about the Mystery Machine. All four had lost something they loved. Was the baron's curse coming true?

Suddenly, Iago appeared. "Come!" he growled. "I take you to castle. Velma now . . . insane!"

"The baron was a genius!" Velma howled. "This monster can be brought to life!"

An angry mob pounded on the door. "We know what you're up to!" the mayor cried.

The townspeople burst in just as —

KA-BLAM! A flash of light exploded.

"It's alive!" Velma shouted. "ALIVE!"

"Get him!" the mayor screamed.

Velma's creature roared. The townspeople turned and ran. The monster chased them.

"You fools! You've ruined everything!" Velma screamed. "Guys, you've got to find my creation."

"Don't worry, Velma," Shaggy said. Suddenly, he felt brave. "Scooby and I will find him."

Daphne and Fred went looking for clues in the castle's secret passageway. It was full of strange mining equipment.

Suddenly, the ghost of the baron appeared! The tunnel began to crumble and cave in. Daphne and Fred were trapped!

Daphne picked up the baron's cape. "If this were the cape of a hundred-year-old baron, it would be real silk. Maybe he's not a ghost!"

Back in the lab, Shaggy and Scooby had found the monster — but Velma had captured them! Her monster needed a brain.

"Where are you going to get a brain?" Shaggy asked.

Velma rolled her eyes. "Between the two of you, you almost have one entire brain. Iago, bring me the brain extractor!"

"Please, Velma," Shaggy yelped. "Don't take our brains. We need what little we have!"

The monster ripped Scooby and Shaggy's new outfits right off their bodies!

"Zoinks!" Shaggy cried. "Hey, I'm starving! Scoob, what are we best at?"

"Reating!" Scooby barked.

The two buddies chewed at the straps tying them down. Soon they were free!

Scooby and Shaggy fled from Velma's monster. They burst into the library.

Shaggy slammed the doors behind them. "Since ol' tall and scaly doesn't have a brain, he probably doesn't have a library card, either."

The two friends blocked off all the entrances to the library. There was just one problem. . . .

"Did we lock the door?" Shaggy asked.

Shaggy and Scooby zoomed out of the library into the same secret tunnel where the baron had trapped Fred and Daphne.

"Red! Raphne!" Scooby barked.

"Like, let's get out of here," Shaggy said.

Just then, a dark shadow crept toward them.

It was Velma! "Come with me if you want to live," she snarled.

Suddenly, Iago appeared. He told the gang the hidden passage was actually a natural gas mining tunnel. "Hurry! We must flee!"

Fred said, "But wait, isn't natural gas —"

"Explosive!" Velma shouted. "We've got to get out of here!" She turned to Shaggy and Scooby. "I'm sorry, guys. I think I was hypnotized."

Scooby and Shaggy shrugged. "Rat's rokay."

The sound of horse hooves came galloping toward them. It was their escape vehicle!

Fred grinned. "Presenting the all-new Mystery Machine."

"Hurry, Fred!" Velma said.

As the carriage burst through the gates, the castle exploded in a giant ball of flame!

Velma's monster was running toward them. Then it stopped — and out jumped Iago!

"Iago," Fred gasped. "You were the monster?"

"No!" Iago pulled off his mask. "I'm Agent Schmidlap from the Department of Defense."

"Wait, you were the monster in the lab?" Shaggy asked.

"No!" the agent said. "That was Burgermeister, the mayor!"

Velma nodded. "This is one mystery that doesn't have a culprit. It has a conspiracy."

"Right," the federal agent said. "That's why they hypnotized you, Velma."

"Who hypnotized you?" Fred wondered.

"And how did Scooby and I become brave — not to mention full?" Shaggy asked.

"This was a personal attack on the Scooby gang!" Velma declared.

Cuthbert Crawley, the lawyer in charge of her uncle's castle, was the first person to blame. "He's really Cuthbert Crawls, the partner of Cosgoode Creeps!"

Shaggy gasped. "They were those creepy lawyers who dressed up as the Green Ghost."

Velma nodded. "Crawley was there to draw us in. The baron's curse was supposed to take away all the things we love the most."

"The first victim? The Mystery Machine, Fred's pride and joy." Velma said. Crawley dressed up as the baron and blew up the van.

Then she turned to the woman who'd sold Daphne her dress. "The next victim was Daphne, who didn't know she was slipping into an inflatable dress!"

"Then Burgermeister gave Shaggy and Scooby their outfits," Velma said. "The lederhosen were designed to make them feel brave and full!"

Shaggy and Scooby grinned. Their tummies growled happily.

"As for me," Velma finished, "Mrs. Vanders hypnotized me into believing I could recreate my uncle's experiment."

"But why?" asked Fred

"It was about us!" said Velma.

"But we don't even know them," said Daphne.

"Don't be so sure," Velma said. She pulled a mask off Burgermeister — it was actually C. L. Magnus, Redbeard's ghost! The woman who sold Daphne her dress was one of Mamba Wamba's zombies. And Mrs. Vanders was Mama Mione, also known as Old Ironface!

"We could have gotten our revenge on you meddling kids!" said Mr. Crawley.

"If it hadn't been for you meddling kids," Mama Mione grumbled.

To thank the gang, Federal Agent Schmidlap gave them one last surprise.

"The Mystery Machine!" Scooby and the gang cheered. "Scooby-Dooby-Doo!"